The Ferret Princess

Tales from the Keep

The Ferret Princess

Joan Lennon   Scoular Anderson

Catnip

CATNIP BOOKS
Published by Catnip Publishing Ltd
14 Greville Street
London EC1N 8SB

First published 2008
1 3 5 7 9 10 8 6 4 2

Text copyright © Joan Lennon 2008
Illustrations copyright ©Scoular Anderson 2008
The moral rights of the author and illustrator have been asserted

A CIP catalogue record for this book is available from the British Library

ISBN 978-1-84647-064-6

Printed in Poland

www.catnippublishing.co.uk

Contents

Chapter One

Trouble and Fuss

I was sitting up on the back battlements in the spring sunshine, swinging my feet over the edge and reading a book, when

the trouble arrived. Not that I *knew* it was trouble. Not right away. Not a clue. I was just sitting, trying to stay out of the way of any chores, thinking deep thoughts like, *I wonder what's for dinner?*

"PRINCESS! PRINCESS! WHERE ARE YOU?!"

When Fat Margaret yells, the sound carries from one end of our very small kingdom to the other. Pretending you haven't heard never works. I didn't even try. I just sighed, and scooped up Jill, my ferret, from the sun-warmed stone, and wrapped her round my neck like a white fur sock. She sighed too, but she didn't bother to wake up.

Fat Margaret had me by the arm before I was halfway down the stairs. (She's called Fat Margaret because she's the skinniest woman you ever saw. But

that doesn't mean she's a weakling —
she's got a grip on her that'd be a credit
to a blacksmith.)

"Quick! On with your ceremonial
dress!"

"*What?!*" I squealed. She'd got me as
far as my room without much fuss, but
now I started to squirm as hard as a
worm in a beak. She *couldn't* be serious
about that dress!

"I can't wear *that!*" I wailed. "It's too
small, *and* it's ugly, and there's a great
big patch at the back where I scorched
it last winter!" (It was so cold that day
that I just kept backing closer and closer
to the fire …) "You mended it with
old *curtains*, for pity's sake — I *can't* wear
that!"

"And you can't wear anything else.
Oh, *don't* be difficult — you'll just have

to keep your back to the wall, or sit down a lot. With your lady mother ill, there's only *you* to receive guests, and there's only *this* to do it in!"

"Mngh? Mnmghmn?" I replied, which translates as "Guests? What guests?" My head was already deep

inside the dress, but that doesn't mean I was happy about wearing it. Though of course she was right. With my mother unable to get up, there was only me to act as hostess. (Everyone insisted she was going to get better, but I tried not to think about it much, because whenever I did I got a tight feeling in my chest.) There are *rules* for royal hostessing – and one of them is that you can't greet guests on behalf of an entire kingdom wearing the same clothes you would to muck out a stable.

But princesses don't muck out stables! I hear you cry.

Well, yes they do, if they're poor enough.

In those days, ours was the poorest castle in the poorest kingdom as far away up in the mountains as it's possible

to get. We were so out of the way, and so hard up, that mostly nobody paid us any heed at all. Conquerors *and* allies didn't really think we were worth the bother. They left us alone, and that suited us fine.

But there's always somebody down-on-their-luck and desperate enough to be jealous even of people like *us*. Somebody who hadn't managed to succeed in the big wide world out

there. Somebody who thought it'd be a doddle, taking a bite out of a no-nothing kingdom, just for starters.

And, as it happened, two of them were waiting downstairs in the Grand Hall at this very moment.

So was I busy making clever political plans? Considering how to meet, greet, and beat dangerous strangers at the game of diplomacy and power?

Not a bit of it. I was fussing about my *dress*.

As I said, I didn't have a clue.

Chapter Two

The Princess in the Picture

If you want to know what I look like, the best idea is probably to go see the painting. The one at the top of the main staircase. It was done a few years back, before my dad died, as a thank-you present from a travelling artist who stayed with us all that wet winter.

Yes, that's me. And I know what you're thinking.

"Doesn't she look like her pet!"

I admit it. Princesses come in all shapes and varieties, from the pink and fluffy, to the ravishing and regal, to the

16

older-than-your-auntie, and everything else besides.

I'm the ferrety sort, and so it's not surprising that they're my favourite animals of all time. (I learned everything I know about them from Warren, our ferreter. He's also our butler and cook and herald and ostler and Jack-of-all-trades and Master-of-pretty-much-all-of-them.)

Ferrets are betwixt-and-between creatures, not quite cats and not quite dogs. They have much more energy than sense, and they over-do *everything*. They love tight places, and sticking their noses where they don't belong, and making a mess of things out of sheer enthusiasm.

And that's pretty much *me*, too. I'm a two-legged, human, right-royal ferret. Well, except for the smell.★ And I don't jump up and down and pull on your breeches when I'm excited. But you get the idea.

★ The thing about ferrets and the way they smell? It's really not that bad – more musky than stinky. To us, I mean. To themselves, of course, *parfum de ferret* is lovely. Very nice indeed. Just right.

A word of warning, though. Don't go upsetting a ferret. If you do, you'll discover … well, just *don't!*

Chapter Three

My Big Entrance

"The news of the queen's illness must have got out," Fat Margaret said as she combed and twisted and generally beat my hair into submission. "They think we're an easy target now. These younger sons – they see their big brothers getting everything and they go all bitter and twisted – or else it's those second-rate nobles - they get greedy where they are, then they get thrown out, then they come looking ..."

With the comb in her mouth it was harder to talk. I shoved in a question.

"How did they get over the border?"

Fat Margaret stuck the comb behind
her ear.

"Don't be stupid, girl. You really think
Old Albert could stop anybody who
wanted to cross? Anyway, he wasn't on

duty today. He was helping Leonard with the spring ploughing."

She gave the dress one more shake to make sure I was thoroughly into it, poked at my hair, and then shoved me in the direction of the Grand Hall.

"Warren will announce you," she hissed. "He's keeping them busy with food till we get there. I'll let him know you're coming." Then she raced off, taking the back way.

No short cuts for me, though. It was through the big double doors, and on down the full length of the great Grand Hall. It was a *long* room – which meant that there was a *lot* of time for our guests to take in all the details of me and my dress. Things like, how very un-pink, un-fluffy, un-regal, and un-ravishing I was. Or how the

only jewellery I was wearing was an unconscious ferret round my neck. Or how old my dress was. Or just exactly how much too small it was. By the time I finally made it to their end of the room I was in such a panic, I felt certain the only question they could possibly have left would be, which room we'd taken the curtains from to patch the back of it with.

"The Third Spare Bedroom," I blurted.

There was a short stunned silence, as the two noble newcomers and their dozen or so attendants all stared. Then Warren waded in with the introductions.

"Allow me," he croaked, coughed, and tried again, "allow me to present Her Highness, the Princess Cecilia, daughter of Their Majesties Queen

Beatrice and the late King Horace of
this realm." He turned and bowed to
me. "Your Highness, may I introduce – "

He got no further. The taller of the two
strangers, lounging against the mantel,
cut across him as if he weren't there.

"I am Count Edward of Frore,"
he said, and then he sniffed. Then he
sniffed *again*, and dabbed at his nose.
It's a definite aroma, ferret, but it was
obviously not one he'd met before.
While I tried to stop turning bright red,

he indicated, as an afterthought, the
other visitor not dressed as a servant.
"And, apparently, that's a Duke of …
someplace or other. We arrived at the
same time."

He would have used the same tone of
voice to say, "He wee'd on my shoe," but
the Duke didn't seem to mind.

"Duke Ferdinand," he said, waving
a cold, cooked chicken leg and not

bothering to get up. "Of the Duchy
of Dram. The, uh, story of your great
beauty reached me, you see, and I had
to, um, I had to … ah, come."

There was an expectant silence from
everyone, but it seemed that was all
the Duke of Dram had to say on the
subject. The fact that my great beauty
was a story didn't appear to trouble him.
Then one of the Duke's company sidled
over and whispered urgently in his ear.

"What?" said the Duke. "You say it's
the mother who's the beauty? Oh well.
Whatever."

He reached for a bit of chicken for
his *other* hand, and carried on stuffing
himself.

If he keeps going at that rate, I thought,
we'll have nothing left for dinner.

Warren must have been thinking

along the same lines, because he
whisked the platter away between one
bite and the next, and quick as a cat,
hid it behind the chair. The Duke kept
chewing, but looked confused.

Not one of Nature's Mighty Minds, I thought to myself. *If I can't handle a wee Dukie-brain like this one, then I should be ashamed of myself.*

Before, I'd been so fussed about myself that I hadn't really *looked* at our guests carefully. But everything I was noticing about Duke Ferdinand now was making me feel more smug and confident by the moment. It seemed to me he was about as noble as my shoe, and as dangerous as that fake jewellery he was wearing – if he thought he could stroll into *my* kingdom and whisk it out from under *me* then he had another think coming and …

I realised Fat Margaret was nudging me, hard, with one of her unnecessarily sharp elbows. The Count was talking again.

"… and since your father the king,"
he was saying, "God rest him, died, I
know how much you and your lady
mother have missed a man's guiding
hand. Women running a kingdom isn't
quite the same, is it, and a *girl* …"

I was all set to get mad, when I
looked him in the eyes – and instantly

31

I was too busy being scared. His eyes were cold, and hard, and hungry, and relentless, and … there was a horrible jolt in my brain as I realised, suddenly, completely, terrifyingly, the danger I was facing.

"When I heard of the queen's unfortunate illness, I felt obliged to pay my respects, along with my servants and all my loyal men-at-arms currently enjoying the hospitality of your peasants …" He shrugged his velvet shoulders and watched me, like some kind of malign spirit.

For one long horrible moment, my
mind shut down. I felt like a rabbit in a
hole, with nowhere to escape to.

The Count didn't move. He went
on leaning against the mantelpiece. It
was as if he knew exactly what I was
feeling, exactly what I was thinking. He
allowed himself a smile, and his teeth
showed little and sharp.

"Er," I said desperately, and stopped.
You could see he was getting pleasure
out of watching me squirm, like a devil
out of hell. Like an evil spirit. Like a …

And then, I remembered something. *Ye Byg Booke of Ghosties and Ghoulies* by Dr Sprout of Brussels (author also of the best-selling *Ye Noble Trials and Tribulations for the Gentrie*) – the book I'd been reading on the battlements that afternoon.

And all at once, I thought I could see a way out.

Chapter Four

The Pink and
The Powerful

There was no time for hesitation – I plunged right in.

"Oh, *sir*," I cooed. "Thank you, thank you! We are so *grateful* to you and this other fine gentleman for showing an interest in little me and my little kingdom. So *few* noblemen these days have the *courage*, the *bravery*, the *fearlessness*, the ..." I'd run out of nouns, but I acted breathless with admiration, instead. I'd seen my cousin Ermintrude do this many times with a great deal of success. "Two rival noblemen, ready to face the *horrors* of the Haunted Tower

– well, in Days of Yore, of course, there would have been *queues* of princes, eager to test themselves – but, sad to say, we live in decadent times …"

I could see Warren and Fat Margaret out of the corner of my eye. Both of them had their mouths hanging open.

"To spend an *entire* night in that *awful* place," I continued, desperately trying to signal to them without the Count or the Duke seeing, "and so earn the right to

rule my realm and perhaps, some day,
my heart – to willingly choose *trial by
ordeal* – oh, gentlemen, I am overcome."
I put a hand to my forehead, and
staggered a little. No effect.

"I said, *I'm overcome!*" I hissed to Fat Margaret, who jumped, shut her mouth, and, *at last*, rushed over to hold me up.

"Warren, get your mistress some water!" she barked. "You know how sensitive she is!" – though I could tell she was really thinking, *You know how crazy she is!*

"What are you talking about? What Haunted Tower? What trial by ordeal?" The Duke sat up straight, sounding panicky.

"Oh sir, it's a fearsome place!" I squeaked, winking wildly at Warren as he handed me a cup, and repeating over and over to myself, *Think fluffy! Think pink!* "Full of Evil Spirits! Rivals who seek to gain the kingdom must first pass the test – the *terrible* test of staying the night in the Tower and wrestling with

Fiends From Hell until the dawn. And all those who fail ..." I dropped my voice for maximum drama "... *are never seen again.*"

The Duke was so agitated he even stopped chewing. "Nobody told *me*

anything about F-f-fiends from Hell!"
he stammered.

"Oh, yes, sir," said Warren, in his best
butler's voice. "Well known that Tower is.
Oh, ghastly things, sir, are told, of what
anyone courageous enough to stay
there might meet – tentacley things, and
slithery things, and headless things, and,
and, strange noises, and er, gurglings,
and …"

Fat Margaret took over. "And the hot
fires of hell that burn you … that burn
you …" she faltered.

"… on the bum!" put in Warren
helpfully.

Fat Margaret glared at him. "On the
nether regions," she corrected primly. "I
understand you can even catch
a whiff of brimstone.
On haunting nights.

When the candidate fails, and is
never seen again. Sirs." And she
dropped a curtsey for good
measure.

All this time, I'd been
afraid to look at the Count,
who was not a fool like the
Duke. But now I did – and immediately
wished I hadn't!

Something had shifted in the
Count's face. It was as if he were seeing
something else, some other scene from
the past, that filled him with … what?
Horror? Fury? It was like looking into
the face of Death … until one of his
servants touched him cautiously on
the arm and he snapped back into the
present again.

"You must take the test," I quavered.
"Or forfeit my hand." *Will I get away*

with it? I wondered. *Why on earth should they agree to any such thing?*

But my luck held. The Count, acting so snooty and superior he was in danger of disappearing up his own nose, nodded. The Duke, not to be left behind, jerked out a "Yes!" as well.

But there was something else on Duke Ferdinand's mind …

For some time now, his eyes had kept flicking nervously to my neck. He was making me self-conscious. I put a hand up and felt … Jill. I'd forgotten she was still there.

Something cracked for the Duke – it seemed he couldn't ignore what his eyes were telling him any longer.

"Your c-collar!" he stammered. "Is it … ? Is it … *breathing?!*"

"Oh sir!" I cried, and I shrank back

a little as if frightened. "What *do* you mean?!"

"Really, Duke, control yourself!" scoffed the Count. He turned and, not bothering to lower his voice, said to one of his servants, "Tell the men they'll be able to move into the castle tomorrow." He strode out of the Hall without a backward glance.

"Yes," said the Duke, trying to sound powerful too, but only succeeding in sounding like a duck. "Yes, tell *my* men that too. About, you know. Tomorrow."

Tomorrow, I thought as I watched him go. *But first we've got … tonight.*

Chapter Five

Scream?

Fat Margaret dragged me into an empty side room and slammed the door.

"Are you *crazy?!*" she hissed. "The Tower's not haunted! And even if it were – did you see the Count's face?! There's something ugly in that man's past, you can mark my words, something that came back to him when you started your nonsense about the Tower. What do you bet he did some awful deed in some similar test, maybe went berserk and killed everyone in sight, including the princess in question – "

"And her faithful hand-maiden too …" muttered Warren.

"Who are you calling a hand-maiden?!" spluttered Fat Margaret, wagging her finger indignantly in his direction.

Jill chose this moment to wake up. She lifted her head, and there was Fat Margaret's finger, wiggling about in front of her nose. So she bit it.

She let go right away, but not before Fat Margaret's remarkable lungs let out on enormous scream.

Almost immediately our unwelcome guests and their followers fell into the room, swords drawn.

"What is it? What's happening? Who screamed?"

"Scream?" said Fat Margaret

innocently, but with her hands carefully behind her back so they wouldn't be able to see the blood. "What scream?"

"*I* didn't hear a scream," I added. I had *my* hands behind my back too. Mine were full of repentant ferret. "Unless – " I let my eyes widen as if in horror " – unless it's started already …"

"What's started already!?" quavered Ferdinand.

"Nothing. Nothing at all," I answered quickly. "Don't worry yourselves, gentle sirs. I'm sure it must have been … it must have been …"

"The wind!" said Fat Margaret. "Must have been." And she nodded emphatically.

At this point, Warren came in.

"Dinner is served," he announced. "Allow me to conduct you to the Dining Chamber, my lords."

"Oh good!" said Duke Ferdinand.

The Count held out an arm to me. "Your Highness?"

I had to think fast.

"Um," I said.

"The Princess will be dining with her

ailing lady mother," said Fat Margaret quickly. "Of course."

The Count looked Fat Margaret up and down. You could tell he didn't much like what he saw. But he didn't say anything. He didn't need to. The man could *look* as much poison as a sackful of snakes. He just turned to me, bowed, and followed his rival out of the room.

Fat Margaret and I each let out ragged breaths.

"Nasty," she said. "Very."

I nodded.

"And you have a plan?"

I nodded again.

"I'll meet you in the Tower, then," she said, "as soon as I can make it. And I'd better bring Warren."

Chapter Six

Ulterior Design

Standing in the middle of the Tower Room, you had to admit it didn't look particularly sinister. Shabby, maybe, and in need of a good spring clean, but haunted?

Oh, dear.

What we had to work with was this: one big bed, three chairs, and a chest full of old clothes waiting to be turned into something else. There was a window with shutters that overlooked the moat far below, and, on the wall, an enormous threadbare tapestry that was so faded you couldn't tell what the

picture was any more. Next to it, there was a fireplace … and that was it.

Jill was exploring the bed, and I was on my knees in front of the chest, grubbing about in it for inspiration, when Warren and Fat Margaret arrived.

"Well?" she said.

"Ah," I said, "when I said I had a plan, I didn't exactly mean a *complete* plan …"

Fat Margaret snorted and started to pace. Warren started to prowl. And I started to throw clothes on the floor in an aimless sort of way.

Jill immediately left the bed and buried herself in the mess. Nose deep in the sleeve of an old gown, tail bushed up and wagging, she went blundering off across Fat Margaret's path, almost sending her flying.

Fat Margaret leapt out of the way, giving a startled squawk, then clapped her hand over her mouth.

"Oh, that beast did give me a fright!" she exclaimed crossly. "Now come *on*, you two – THINK!"

There was a short pause.

"Think," I said vaguely.

"Think," said Warren absently.

"YES!!" scolded Fat Margaret. "Stop being useless and help me figure out *how* on earth we are going to rig this room up in any way whatsoever scary enough to spook two grown greedy dangerous nasty … ARE YOU LISTENING TO ME?!?"

We weren't.

I was staring at Warren. Warren was

staring at me.

"And we have … how many ferrets in the busyness★ just now?" I asked, trying to sound casual.

Warren counted on his fingers. "There's Frank and Hob and Big Bob

and Jeremy and Sable and Kevin, and Cynthia and Katie and Jenny and

★A group of ferrets is called a busyness. Who says there's no truth in advertising?!

Pinkums, and Jill, of course, and wee Emily. That's twelve."

"A dozen ferrets," I said.

"That's right," he said.

"Should be enough," I said.

"I'll go fetch some treats," he said.

"WHAT IS GOING ON???" said Fat Margaret through clenched teeth.

I went over and patted her on the shoulder.

"Trust me," I said. "I'm a princess."

Chapter Seven

Trials and Tribulations for the Gentrie

When bedtime for the noblemen came,
Warren and I were out of sight, hidden
behind the tapestry. Nothing could
begin until they were asleep, but Duke
Ferdinand was so busy babbling that
that might not be for some time. He
kept boasting about how fantastically
fearless he was and then wondering if
the Tower really *could* be haunted, but
the Count didn't deign to answer him.
He didn't say anything at all until, in a
rare pause for breath by the Duke, we
heard his voice, low and cold.

"They'll pay for this."

Just four words – but they made my heart stutter.

They must have had an effect on the Duke as well, because he stopped rabbitting. Not long afterwards the candles were blown out and the bed creaked.

We waited. And waited. And waited.

The stillness seemed to go on forever until, finally, Warren peered out around the edge of the tapestry.

"All right," he whispered. "They're asleep. Let's go."

We tiptoed about in the dying firelight, laying out articles of clothing with the sleeves and legs tied at the ends, and tasty bits of food stuffed inside. Some were on the floor. Some were on the chairs. I hung a gown from a hook

behind the door and put treats in its pockets. It was long past ferret teatime, and even if it weren't, we knew full well that not one of our beasts could resist the challenge of a tidbit, just out of reach, at the end of anything even remotely tunnel-like. There were eager scuffling noises from inside the chest, where the entire busyness of hungry ferrets had been hidden.★ As a final touch, Warren stirred up the fire and draped a thin piece of worn-out scarlet cloth from the mantel, so that the room was now bathed in a ghastly glow. Then we scurried back behind the tapestry,

★ Don't worry. It's a thing about ferrets that they like having at least one more of themselves in a space than will sensibly fit. Even so, don't try this at home.

flipping open the lid of the chest as we passed, and MOANED!

The two noblemen sat bolt upright in the bed. As their eyes snapped open they saw, to their horror, strange

shapes racing about the room, lit by an unearthly redness. The shapes chittered and squeaked like wingless bats out of hell – and then *disappeared!* In their place, larger creatures appeared, with oddly shaped bodies wearing tunics and breeches and shoes that juddered and twitched, then slithered about on the floor in different directions. In the doorway, something wearing a dress danced and swayed wildly. Everywhere there were headless apparitions falling apart in front

of their eyes and making horrible
muffled gargling sounds …

"It's the demons!" shrieked
the Duke. "They've come to
get me!" And he tried to leap into
the Count's arms.

Count Edward snarled and pushed
him away. The Duke whimpered and
dived under the blankets. The Count's
face was twisted and his teeth showed in
the strange light, but he showed no sign
of budging.

It wasn't working! Instead of running
out of the room yelling, one of them
was so scared he was practically
inside the mattress, and the other
wasn't anywhere near scared *enough*.
Warren and I looked at each other in
desperation – what more could we do?

Then, amidst the demonic chuckling

and chattering and writhing, we heard something else – another sound, one that was growing in volume all the time. It was a *hissing*, followed by a *bump, bump*.

The Count's eyes swivelled in his head, trying to locate this new horror. From the edge of the tapestry we did the same, because a hissing ferret is not a happy one. And then we spotted her.

It was Emily. She was the youngest of the busyness, barely more than a kit, and, in spite of having a heart full of courage, she was not very big and not very strong.

She'd managed to get herself completely tangled in an old pair of breeches, *and* she had run them and herself into a corner, *and* no matter how hard she thrashed and squirmed, she couldn't get at the treat and she couldn't get out. She just kept banging into the wall, getting more and more frustrated.

Then the Count did something we hadn't expected. He stood up – *and he was holding his sword!*

He must have had it in bed with him. Suddenly Fat Margaret's guess about the Count slaughtering princesses in the past seemed not so unbelievable. And, as luck would have it, this was the moment Emily finally made her escape. She'd managed to get her head out of the breeches. The first thing that met her eyes was a complete stranger, creeping towards her with a drawn sword.

She *screeched*.

It was a noise that made every adult ferret in the room freeze in its tracks. It was a noise that made the Duke of Dram burrow even deeper under the bedclothes, wailing as he went. But the Count –

 – just kept on creeping.

He was bending right over now, trying in the dim light to identify what it was he was seeing, there on the floor.

There was no chance this was something he was going to get away with.

There was a tremendous scrabbling of claws and ripping of old clothes from every part of the room. Some of the busyness headed straight for Emily, got her out of the breeches, scruffed her and dragged her away to safety. The rest turned their attention to THE THREAT. As one, they leapt into the air and sank a multitude of needle-sharp teeth into that bit that sticks out the most, when a Count (or anybody else for that matter) bends way over …

They bit him right on *the Nether Regions!*

"Help! Help! My bum's on fire!" shrieked the Count. "*They got me!*"

Ferdinand peeked out from under the pillows. By now the Count was spinning round like a crazy thing, batting at his backside with a great flailing of bony arms and flapping nightshirt. It was impossible to *see* what was happening to him, but Ferdinand had no trouble with another of his senses.

"PEE-YEWWW!!" he gasped.

The Duke fell out of the bed and staggered back against the far wall, holding his sleeve over his nose and mouth and gagging.

"EUGGHHH! Heaven preserve us – it must be … IT'S THE STINK OF HELLLL!!" he gargled. With his free hand he began to fumble wildly with the shutters – he wrenched them open at last –

– and leapt straight out the window!

I *screamed*. I couldn't help it! I'm pretty sure Warren screamed too. That may have been the last straw for the Count – I don't know. Because then *he did it too!*

Nightshirt flapping, arms windmilling, and with a bunch of fully bushed-up ferrets attached to his backside like the tail to a comet, Count Edward of Frore staggered across to the window and *dived*.

Chapter Eight

What Happened Next ...

Warren and I raced to the window and leaned out.

Far below, there was something thrashing in the moat. *Two* somethings,

which eventually floundered over to the edge, dragged themselves out, and ran off, gibbering, into the moonlight. And then ...

... the sound of delighted chittering drifted up to us. There, messing about in the water, as if they went flying off tall towers attached to strangers every day of the week, were the ferrets.

Warren let a whoop of relief and raced off down the stairs to collect them.

Smiling insanely, I set about doing the same with the rest of the busyness. Finding and bagging a lot of over-excited ferrets is not the job of a moment, but I managed it at last, just as Warren returned.

I turned to him, happy and triumphant.

"And I found Hob, and Big Bob, and
Cynthia and Jenny," he said. "Down
by the moat. They're not hurt. Just a bit
crazy. Like after a bath."

Then he paused, and the look on his face made me feel as if I'd swallowed my heart.

"And Frank and Sable and Jeremy and Emily – I've got them here," I said breathlessly. "They're fine – look – they're fast asleep already – it was just a game to them – really it was …"

He nodded. "And Katie and Pinkums were chasing Kevin about on the staircase as I came up." He stopped.

"And?" My voice sounded wrong.

Warren didn't seem to want to look at me.

"AND?" I shouted.

"It's Jill," he said. "Where's Jill."

Suddenly it was all more

than I could bear. It had been just too long a day and too crazy a night and I'd almost killed two people and now it looked as if I *had* killed my best ferret-friend and it had all seemed like such a good idea at the time …

Suddenly I just wanted my mum.

Chapter Nine

The White One?

I blundered along the corridor with no thought to how late it was, and piled straight into Fat Margaret's skinny arms. She was just coming out of my mother's room. She took one look at me, and said,

"Go on in with you then. She's not asleep."

There she was, sitting up in bed and smiling at me, and before I knew it I was scrunched up beside her, telling her everything – all about the nasty Count and the feeble Ferdinand and my plan to scare the pants off them and how it

worked so well and then it worked *too*
well and then it all went wrong and
I hadn't even known that ferrets *could*
swim before but then Jill … and now
Jill …

"Is Jill the big one, with the white
fur?"

My mother's voice was too soft, too
calm.

 "And the red eyes?" she
continued. "And the broken
claw on her right front
foot …"

I looked at her in surprise.
Jill had only broken that
claw this morning. She'd been trying
to dig one of her toys out from a stone
gutter she'd wedged it into. How could
my mother possibly have known about
that?

"Yes, but how …" I started to ask her,
but the look on her face stopped me
with an impossible hope.

"… like that?"

She was pointing to the foot of the
bed. There was only a single candle
burning in the room, so at first it was
hard to see what she was pointing *at*.
But then my eyes cleared and I realised

that what had looked like a lump in the
bedclothes was, in fact, blinking sleepily
at me.

It was Jill. And she was not alone.

She was curled around a heap of tiny
brand-new kits. She'd been giving birth
while the rest of us had been playing
the fool.

Suddenly, there was a gigantic honk that made all of us jump. *What now?!* I thought. But it was only Fat Margaret, standing by the door, blowing her nose.

"I'll just go and tell Warren," she muttered gruffly. "Silly boy's mad about the beasts …"

She was trying so hard not to look soft – you had to laugh.

I snuggled in with my mum at the top end of the bed, and Jill and her babies went back to sleep at the bottom end, and it was big sighs of content all round.

"So, my ferret-girl," said my mother softly, "it's all worked out, after all."

I'm almost positive it was Jill she was talking to …

If you enjoyed *The Ferret Princess* you'll love the other book in the Tales from the Keep series, *Wag and the King*. Read on for a sample.

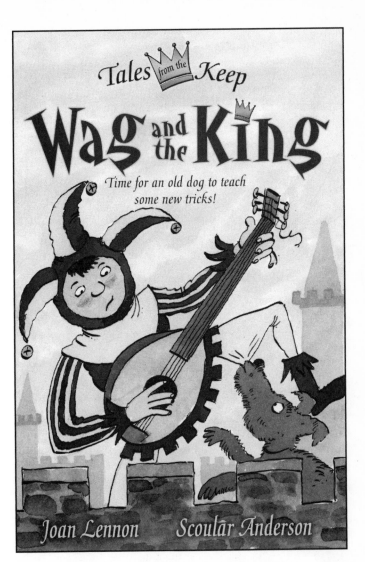

Tales from the Keep

Wag and the King

Time for an old dog to teach
some new tricks!

Joan Lennon   Scoular Anderson

Chapter One

Old Dog, New Tricks?

Remember that thing they say?

You can't teach an old dog new tricks.

Ever stop to wonder *why*? If you did, you probably thought it was because old dogs are too stupid, or old dogs are too stiff. Rubbish! Old dogs can't learn new tricks because *they haven't got the time!*

My Name's Wag. I'm old, and I'm a dog. And I am SO BUSY keeping my human out of trouble that I have NO TIME LEFT to learn tricks. Old tricks, new tricks, tricks of *any* sort or smell.

Oh, come on, you say. No one can get in *that* much trouble, you say. You *must* be exaggerating.

That's what you say.

Are you right? I don't think so. Take last week, for example …

Chapter Two

Apprentice Tom

The Boy's name is Tom, and I've had him ever since his parents left him here, at the Castle, when he was little more than a puppy.

Do you know about apprenticing? If you do, you can skip the rest of this bit. If you don't – this is how it works.

Humans with a big litter apprentice some of them to other humans (called Masters) who are skilled at something the parents don't know much about themselves. The children learn a new trade by watching and helping and being taught, and the Master gets a new assistant. Even the Princes and Princesses get sent away to other castles, to learn things about Kinging and Queening that maybe their own mothers and fathers aren't so good on. It's a pretty sensible system, and mostly it all works out quite well.

Mostly.

In Tom's case, his parents apprenticed him to the Court Minstrel. On the face of it, they couldn't have chosen a better job for their son: no heavy lifting, indoor work, guaranteed invitations to every feast, nice clothes and a warm basket, er, bed to sleep in. The Master Minstrel was one of the Old King's favourites. The Old King died not so long ago, and his son Roderick was called back from *his* apprenticeship to take over. So now we have a Young King. He's still new at the job and has a lot to learn, but he seems a likeable enough human. *And* he seems to be perfectly happy with his father's Minstrel, so that should be good news for the Boy, too.

It sounds great, doesn't it?

As it worked out, however, it was a bit like apprenticing a Jack Russell to an Irish Wolfhound.

Not exactly the perfect match, if you get what I mean.

Chapter Three

Minstrel Mismatch

"You CANNOT sing an Ode to the Beauty of Lady Gravel with your eyes crossed and pretending to be sick all the time!" the Master shouted.

"You cannot sing an Ode to the Beauty of Lady Gravel AT ALL!" the Boy shouted back. "Because the Beauty of Lady Gravel doesn't exist!!"

There you have it. It's not that Tom can't sing – he has quite a nice voice, and we've had many a pleasant howl together of an evening. But when it comes to flattering the Lords and Ladies of the Court with flowery phrases, or complimenting all the Royal Relatives in rhyming couplets, or warbling "The Lament of Lord Stush" – well, as far as *that* part of the job goes, the Boy hasn't the nose for it, and no mistake.

Lord Pompadour his foes did ravage …

… **He's** no more savage than a cabbage !

How rare a gem is our Monarch's Auntie …

… Her bulk is vast, and her brains are scanty !

The Lord, a-weltering in his blood,
Took a long last look at his Lady
And murmured, 'My Dearest, oh my, ah me!

When I'm dead, dear Lady, remember me!'

And she looked at him, and sighed,

and said,

"All right, but I really do **not** suppose

That you're going to die,

With a slight black eye

And a great big fat bloody nose!"

You get the idea.

In the course of this morning alone, the Boy had already had a scroll, a roll, and a flagon thrown at him by the Master.

"GET OUT GET OUT GET OUT!" bellowed the Master. "And take that mangy mongrel with you!"

Tom grinned at me. Escape! But then the Master changed his mind.

"NO!" he yelled. "Come back. I've got a better idea."

Oh-oh. The Boy and I exchanged worried looks.

"You can attend the King's Audience instead. And you can *stay there* until you find something *you* deem worthy of singing an Ode about. Don't come back without a finished song. And take the dog."

He could be really mean, the Master.

So there we were, stuck in the Great Hall, listening to a bunch of old poops droning on about drains and taxes and treaties and trade. The only person more bored than us was the Young King. He kept yawning behind his hand, and playing with his sleeves. (Great long droopy sleeves-to-the-floor was one of the idiot fashions he'd brought back from his apprenticeship at Castle Finicky.) He looked really silly, and really fed up.

Until … there was a blare of trumpets

that made everybody jump. They only use the trumpets to announce the arrival of *really important* people. So who important would want to show up to an event as dull as this one? I wondered.

I was just about to find out – and when I did, I couldn't stop my tail from wagging like a windmill.